CW01431919

The Harmony Inn Homicide

A Very Merry Murder Mystery, Volume 4

Rachel Beattie

Published by Rachel Beattie, 2024.

THE HARMONY INN HOMICIDE

First edition. October 11, 2024.

Copyright © 2024 Rachel Beattie.

ISBN: 979-8227321251

Written by Rachel Beattie.

Chapter One

"Well, it ain't good news, Mrs...ah...Ms..."

"Merry." I lock my smile in place and try to resist the urge to remind Bill Hughes - owner and proprietor of *Bill the Bug Guy*, Silver Brook's premier pest control company - that he's known me for at least a decade. He was once on a bowling team with my ex-husband. "Just call me Merry."

"Right. Merry." He shoots me a relieved grin, then looks down at the scrap of paper he's been furiously scribbling on since he stepped across the threshold of my poor, suffering home. "It looks like an infestation and that isn't going to be an easy job to fix. Or a quick one." He pauses and I'm pretty sure his grin widens. "Or a cheap one." He passes me the piece of paper. "Here's what you're looking at for me to sort the problem for you." He taps the larger of the two massive figures he's worked out for me. "This much if it's a rush job."

"I see." The edges of my vision blacken and I'm pretty sure I see stars for a minute. This is going to pretty much clear out my emergency savings but I suppose if anything qualifies as an emergency it's termites threatening to destroy my house. "And is there any way I can pay in installments?"

"Huh?"

I pass the scrap of paper back to him.

"I could give you a deposit to get the work started, then make payments on the rest?" I swallow, forcing my voice to soften. "For old times' sake?"

"Well..." Bill scratches his chin. "I don't usually do things that way...I mean, there's a lot of upfront costs to me, y'see, and..."

"Fine." My smile stretches painfully across my face. "No problem. I can make it work." *Maybe I can sell a kidney or something.* Something soft thumps into the back of my leg, making my knee give and I bend down to see Snuffy, my cat, winding himself around my ankles.

"You'll have to move out, too. And take the cat with you." Bill gestures towards Snuffy, who sniffs and continues to paw at my feet. "I'll probably need to tent the place and that isn't great for people. Or animals." He glances around the room, eyeing several leggy houseplants. "Or living things in general." He shrugs. "It'll take about a week."

"A week?" I bend down and scoop Snuffy into my arms. "Where am I supposed to go?"

Bill looks momentarily horrified as if I've asked him to put us up and I shake my head, forestalling his panic.

"I'm just thinking out loud."

"Most people go and stay with family. Friends." He shrugs. "Surely there's someone in town with a spare room you can stay in."

I nod but privately I'm not so sure. The two people I'd usually ask - my best friends Jeremy and Kate - are currently out of town on a romantic getaway together. There's my boyfriend, but we're not exactly at the living-together stage in our relationship just yet. Snuffy squirms, reminding me of the other, major, reason staying at Rob's is an impossibility. He has two very large, very soppy, but very decidedly un-cat-friendly dogs.

"Well, I'd better get going," Bill says. "You have my number if you need to ask me anything else. If you want to go ahead with the work just call and we'll get things moving." He leans over and tentatively scratches Snuffy behind the ears. "Just don't take too long. With problems like this, they only get worse, the longer you leave 'em." He winks, and I know at least some of the *worse* is *more expensive*. I can practically hear my bank account dwindling to zero with every second that ticks by.

"I'll give you a call later today. Tomorrow at the latest," I promise. "Just as soon as I sort a few details out."

I show him out and shut the door, surveying the house as if it isn't currently trying to drive me insane. I've always loved this place but lately it's starting to feel like it might be a little cursed. It began with a leaking faucet that I bravely assured my helpful boyfriend that I was more than capable of fixing myself. My foray into feminism meant an emergency late-night call to a plumber and cost me twice as much as if I'd let Rob look at it, to begin with. Then there was the intermittent electrical fault that had things switching themselves on and off at odd hours of the day and night. Once lights started flickering and I'd convinced myself the house was haunted the problem was proved to be faulty wiring, which was a little easier to fix than a resident ghost might have been. And then came the termites.

"Oh well," I say to Snuffy. "If bad luck comes in threes I guess we're well and truly out of the woods after this." Which is good, because if anything else needs fixing around here I'll need to start paying for it with my good looks and that isn't going to get me very far. "Right, you." I drop Snuffy down on the sofa and grab my purse and keys, making for the door. I left my friend Phoebe to open up the Jitterbug Junction today so I could stay home and speak to Bill, but I promised her I wouldn't leave her flying solo in the café for long. I certainly can't afford for anything to go wrong with the business now I'm about to fork out all my available cash to keep my house standing. I give Snuffy one last pet and head out, driving the short distance to the center of Silver Brook while I think over my options. I can't stay with Kate and Jeremy. I shouldn't stay with Rob - even though I'm sure he'd find some way to make it work if I needed him to. There must be another option. The idea hits me as I roll into my usual parking space. It'll mean more money, but it'll also enable me to keep a little bit more of my independence while my house is out of action. The Harmony Inn. Silver Brook's best - and only - Bed and Breakfast is sure to have a room I can use for the week or so I need somewhere else to stay. I bite my lip. I'll just have to see if I can persuade Hannah Kincaid to let me bring Snuffy with me...

• • • •

"NO ANIMALS."

I'd thought it was a sign from the universe when Hannah herself came into the Jitterbug Junction for her morning latte, and even though she was surrounded by other members of the Silver Brook Sewing Circle, I took my chance and asked about a room at the inn that's been in her family for generations.

"Oh, but Snuffy's more than just an animal." I smile. "He's practically human. He's so well-behaved, and -"

"No animals." Hannah frowns at me, then slowly puts down her needle and thread to free up her hands for counting. "No animals. No smoking. No drinking. No members of the opposite sex in your room unless you are married." She purses her lips. "To that person, I mean."

I nod, tugging nervously on one of my favorite beaded earrings.

"Meals need to be booked in advance, and mealtimes will be strictly observed." She arches a penciled-on eyebrow. "I know it sounds strict, but believe me, I'm a lot more relaxed than my Ma used to be."

"Not your grandmother, though."

"Hush!" Hannah silences one of her sewing-circle friends with a look then turns back to me, her scowl melting into a smile. "I'd love for you to come stay with us, Meredith, dear." Her smile drops. "Providing you can keep to those few simple rules."

"Of course!" I nod and repeat them back to show how keenly I was listening. "No pets. No smoking or drinking. Nobody else in my room but me." I smile. "And book meals in advance."

"She would be allowed to bring that handsome young man of hers to dinner though, wouldn't she?" Another of the sewing circle ladies beams at me. "He'd certainly brighten up the place."

"Jean Montrose, if you have complaints about the way I run the Harmony Inn you're more than welcome to find somewhere else to live." Hannah huffs, returning to her sewing and running several quick, tight stitches without pausing for breath.

"As if you'd ever manage to run that place without me there to help." Jean chuckles, entirely undeterred by her old friend. "You can hardly even manage the staff! I heard you arguing with Delphine this morning. What did she want, a pay increase?"

"Never you mind." Hannah shoots Jean a quelling look. "Delphine needs to remember her place, that's all. She can't go around threatening -"

"Threatening?" Jean laughs. "Goodness me, you make it all sound so intriguing! As if mousy little Delphine could ever threaten anyone with anything other than a spilled drink." She turns to me. "Don't let Hannah put you off. Harmony Inn is near enough half mine, anyway. You come and stay for as long as you want, Merry. You'd be more than welcome."

"I didn't say she wasn't!" Hannah smiles at me. "You're very welcome to come and stay in my inn, Meredith." She puts a subtle, but unmissable emphasis on *my inn* and I see Jean's face fall. Hannah continues, oblivious. "I'll put you in the blue room. It's not quite the best room in the house, but unfortunately we have quite a few other guests with us at present, so -"

"I'm sure it'll be lovely," I say quickly, inwardly rejoicing that I've managed to solve my housing problem so quickly and easily. Relatively speaking. "Thank you so much. I'll need to make a few more arrangements but I will probably come tomorrow, if that's alright?"

"Very well. You'll need to check in before noon."

"Thank you." My gaze travels past Hannah to Jean, who is smiling again as if she hadn't felt the weight of her cousin's snub a few minutes earlier. "Thank you very much." With one last check on the table to ensure everyone has everything they need, I wander back to the counter, where Phoebe is cleaning and pretending not to eavesdrop on our conversation.

"What was that about?" she asks, in a low, curious voice.

"Just me giving my last dime to Hannah Kincaid." I groan, then fill Phoebe in on my morning. "Bill wants to tent my house which means Snuffy and I need to find somewhere else to stay for a week." I sigh. "I'm sorted now, thank goodness, but my cat…"

"He can stay with me." Phoebe acts as if this is a foregone conclusion. "I mean, my place isn't very big, but I'm more than happy to take him in for a few days."

"Really?" I give her an impromptu hug. "That would be great. Rob said he'd find space for him at the vet's clinic if there was no other option but I hate to think of him locked away in a cage all week."

"Oh, at mine he'll have the run of at least one whole room." Phoebe laughs. She currently rents a small studio apartment and I know she'd like to eventually find somewhere bigger.

"Thank you."

"No problem." Phoebe tosses a cleaning rag at me. "After all, I kind of owe you. If it wasn't for you I wouldn't have that place to begin with. Or this job." She smiles and we both remember the tragedy that brought Phoebe to Silver Brook to begin with. I'm so glad she stayed. She's been an asset to the Jitterbug Junction and is well on her way to becoming one of my closest friends. "Only, I should probably warn you about the Harmony Inn..."

"What about it?" My heart sinks. Phoebe stayed at the inn for a few weeks when she first arrived in Silver Brook. If anyone's going to have a decent insight into the place, it's her.

"Hannah isn't joking about the rules. Break them and you're out. And she and Jean squabble but they back each other up when it counts." She smiles. "If you want to make Hannah squirm, get Jean talking about the history of the place. They're cousins, you know, and the inn originally belonged to their great-grandmother." She pauses. "Or maybe there's another great in there. I don't know. Anyway, it's as old as the hills and has a history to match, which for some reason Hannah Kincaid is not all that fond of talking about."

"Is that so?" I risk a glance back at the sewing circle to see half a dozen greying heads bent over their work. Everyone is smiling and chatting merrily except for Hannah, who continues to scowl as she works tiny, neat stitches. If she runs her business the same way she handles a needle it looks like my week could be more than a little tense. It might be handy to have a weapon or two at my disposal. "I'll bear that in mind."

Chapter Two

"You know I would have been happy to put you up." Rob reaches across me into the carton of popcorn I'm holding on my lap and grabs a sugary handful. "We could have figured something out." He smiles at me. "You like dogs, right?"

"I like your dogs. Aren't you also watching a couple for a friend?" I turn my phone on silent while we wait for the movie to start. Silver Brook's ramshackle old movie theater is undergoing something of a revival lately, and I settle back into the surprisingly comfortable seats. "You still haven't told me about the new pair. What are you training them for?" I smile, thinking of cute videos of guide dog puppies I've seen online. "I bet they're adorable."

"Ha!" Rob grins. "Yeah, something like that. Let's just say my small house feels a lot smaller with these additions. It's probably a good thing you aren't going to have to fight them for space on the sofa."

"Exactly. This is the best option for everyone. Phoebe is going to look after Snuffy and I'll get to stay at the Harmony Inn. I'm kind of looking forward to it."

"Really?" He eyes me and reaches for the popcorn again and I frown, silently pointing out that we aren't going to have any left for the movie if he eats it all before the trailers even start. He winks and picks out just one kernel he pops into his mouth before speaking again. "You can handle a whole week of Jean Montrose and Hannah Kincaid sniping at each other over the breakfast table?"

"How do you know about that?"

"I have my sources." He waggles his eyebrows at me but can only hold his peace for a minute. "My friend Chris is staying there for a few days while we work on training up these dogs. You'll like her."

Her? When Rob had mentioned his *work friend Chris* I'd thought *she* was a guy. I don't have time to do more than digest this key detail before the overhead lights dim and the tinny speakers of Silver Brook's vintage movie theater screech into life.

I'm soon sucked into an old black-and-white tale of intrigue and family secrets so tangled I can barely keep track of who's who, never mind whodunnit, and when the credits roll and the lights come back on I'm still scratching my head.

"So?" Rob nudges me. "What did you think?"

"I liked it!" I frown. "But I still don't get it."

"What? I was hoping you could explain it to me!" He plucks the empty popcorn container from my lap, guiding me out of the theater and into the dark Silver Brook street.

"Where am I dropping you? Your house? Or your new home from home?"

"Better take me to the inn," I say, with a wistful look out of the window. "I dropped my things off there earlier and just had enough time to tell Hannah I wouldn't be joining them for dinner before I came to meet you."

"So you haven't met any of the regulars yet?" Rob grins. "You have a treat in store."

There's something about the amusement in my boyfriend's voice that makes me think his definition of "treat" and mine differ wildly.

"I haven't met Chris yet either," I remind him. "Your friend." I pause but he doesn't take the hint. "So, tell me about her. Do you guys go way back?"

"Way." He nods. "We were at college together."

"Oh?" I try to keep my voice neutral but something must have given me away because Rob glances at me, his smile dropping just a little.

"We were *friends* at college together. She's like a sister to me." He pulls a face. "And you know I already have plenty of those." Rob adores his two sisters, even though the way he jokes about them would make a person think otherwise. "Chris has all brothers, so I think we just fell into that kind of relationship with each other. You'll like her," he insists. "And she can't wait to meet you."

"Oh." My stomach drops. *I hope she isn't expecting too much*. It's not like I'm a nightmare to get on with, at least I don't think so, but I'm also tired and cranky and worried about my house. If the first time I'm going to meet Chris is over the breakfast table - before my first coffee of the day - then I'm bound to be a disappointment.

"I'm more interested in getting your take on the rest of the people staying there," Rob continues, oblivious to my anxieties. "Hearing some of Chris's stories makes it sound like quite the collection of oddballs." He starts counting them off as he drives. "There's Jean and Hannah you already know, of course, then this older couple who come and stay every year for their anniversary."

"That's nice," I interject.

"It is." He nods. "And a guy called Edward...Edmund...Ed-something, who's super quiet and bookish and intense - don't ask him for help with a crossword or you'll never get away."

"Good to know." I'm not a big crossword person, but I file that one away for future reference.

"And Chris." He glances at me with a grin. "And now you. Pretty crowded, if you ask me. The Harmony Inn isn't that big."

"I won't be there much," I say, reassuring myself as much as him. "I'm still going to be working most of the time." I muster a smile as he turns onto the winding, climbing road that will lead to my new home for the next several days. "And who knows, maybe Bill will get my house sorted out quicker than he estimates. I'll be back home before I know it."

"You will." Rob nods. "And if the inn and its inhabitants get too much to bear before then, you can always come and stay with me. I'm sure we can persuade the dogs to give up the sofa. Or at least agree to share it."

· · · ·

MY ROOM AT THE INN may have suffered from a floral chintz explosion, but the bed is actually pretty comfortable, and without Snuffy noisily demanding his breakfast I sleep right through my alarm, waking up to bright sunlight shining through a crack in the curtains.

"What time is it?" I mutter, clutching at my phone and letting out a yelp as I see just how late I've slept. I jump out of bed and wriggle into my clothes, pausing at the washstand - a quaint attempt to offset the single, shared bathroom offered at the inn - to splash cold water on my face before running downstairs and into my day.

"Meredith!"

"Merry, dear! Is that you?"

One sharp voice and another softer one stops me in my tracks and I backtrack enough to poke my head into the breakfast room to see a large square table laden with food and surrounded by people. There's just one free chair and it looks like, as far as Hannah and Jean are concerned, it has my name on it.

"I'm sorry I'm late," I gulp. "I slept in, and now I need -"

"To sit down and eat your breakfast," Hannah says, in a tone of voice that won't be argued with. I consider trying, but Jean shakes her head gently, out of sight of her cousin, and I decide the last thing I need right now is to get into an argument.

"Well, only if you're sure there's enough to go around," I say, carefully squeezing through the narrow gap between the table and the wall to find my place. "Good morning." I blush, realizing just how many curious pairs of eyes are fixed on me, and I'm relieved when conversations start up again, first in whispers, then gradually with more enthusiasm.

"Morning." A pretty blonde woman next to me passes me the coffee pot with a grin. "You look like you need this."

"Thank you!" I gratefully pour myself a cup and take a mouthful before adding cream and sugar. "I missed my alarm."

"That's what you get for going to the midnight show at the movie theater." Her eyes sparkle with amusement. "Did you figure out who the killer was?"

I'm nonplussed. I'm pretty sure I've never met this woman and I have no idea how she knows what I was doing last night. Realization dawns at the moment she nudges me with her shoulder.

"Rob told me. I'm Chris!"

"Chris." The word tastes like sawdust, and my smile, which had been effortless, now feels heavy. "Merry. It's nice to meet you."

"You too!" Chris helps herself to a slice of toast and spreads a thick layer of blackberry jelly on it before taking a bite. "I've heard so much about you!"

I keep my smile in place but inwardly my heart is thumping. I've met a few of the people in Rob's life - his sisters and their families - but college friends are new territory, and I can't help but feel awkward and uncomfortable. *It doesn't help that she looks like the cover model from Healthy Outdoor Pursuits Monthly.* I veto my original planned breakfast and opt for cereal and fruit instead of sausage, heaping a dull bowlful of the stuff before taking a large, tasteless mouthful.

"So what are you doing today?" Chris asks, oblivious to my misery. "I was hoping we could spend some time together. I'd love to get to know you a little better. You're important to Rob, and he's important to me, so..."

"I have to work," I say, swallowing a flavorless lump of fiber. "All day. Very busy." She looks disappointed and I manage a smile that's almost genuine. "I'm sorry."

"Meredith works at the best cafe in town, don't you dear?" Jean beams at me across the table. "You should give it a visit, Chris. You'll love it."

"Oh yeah? That sounds great."

"We'll definitely pop in!" A cheery voice adds to our conversation and I see two identical smiles on two disturbingly similar faces on my right. "We can't wait to see what you've done with the place."

"That's right. We used to visit all the time back when Maggie was in charge, didn't we darling?"

"Certainly did, darling. It was our favorite part of coming to visit Silver Brook." The female half of the couple blanches, then recovers. "Apart from staying here, of course."

Hannah harrumphs and tops up her tea from a china pot she guards as if it's the crown jewels of England.

"Well, Maggie certainly did a great job of running the Jitterbug," Jean says. "But it's going from strength to strength now with Merry at the helm."

"I try," I say, with a small smile. "It helps that everyone is still so loyal."

"And you don't have much in the way of competition."

A stiff, robotic voice pipes up from one corner of the table and I glance over to see a thin, middle-aged man with glasses and thinning grey hair tied into a low ponytail bent over a book. He turns a page without looking up and continues his observation.

"The Jitterbug Junction is the only cafe in a three-mile radius. It was established fifty years ago as Mabel's Moon Pie Diner. The Jitterbug name didn't come until much later."

I exchange a look with Chris, who seems to be trying especially hard not to laugh.

"Thank you, Edgar. We can always rely on you to share a fascinating detail of Silver Brook's history with us. Merry," Jean turns to me. "Edgar is writing a history of the town. He's been making his way around this part of the country researching small-town America for - how long has it been now?"

"Five years." Edgar turns another page, apparently oblivious to the looks he's getting from the rest of us. "Silver Brook has some interesting history several generations back, including this very inn, which -"

"Well, I'm sure everyone has plans for the day. We oughtn't to waste time lingering over breakfast. Delphine!" Hannah claps her hands and a small, mousy young woman appears like a shadow in the doorway. She doesn't look at all like the Delphine I'd imagined when I heard Hannah and Jean discussing her at the cafe. The maid obediently begins clearing the table without further instruction and I only just manage to hang onto my coffee cup, though I'm more than happy to surrender my half-eaten bowl of cereal and fruit to her eager hands. If she really did try to extract higher wages from her employers, it doesn't seem like she succeeded. I wonder if Hannah's sharp temper was enough to put her back in her place.

"So, the Jitterbug Junction?" Chris asks, in a low enough whisper that it shouldn't carry to our neighbors' ears.

"On the high street," I nod, swallowing the last of my drink. "You can't miss it."

"I certainly don't intend to!" She beams at me. "I'll see you there later today, and hopefully we can have some proper getting-to-know-you time."

I nod, but certainly can't match her enthusiasm. *She's Rob's friend*, I remind myself. *You need to make an effort. He gets on well with Jeremy and Kate, why can't you do the same with Chris?* I sigh. *Because*, I argue internally, *Jeremy and Kate don't look like they belong on the front page of a fashion magazine.*

Chapter Three

It's a busy day at the Jitterbug Junction with half of Silver Brook coming in and out. I'm so snowed under making and fulfilling orders that it takes a while for me to notice that one of the people lingering over coffee and pastries certainly has somewhere else he ought to be. I grab a coffee pot and storm over to his table.

"Good afternoon, Bill." I lift the pot, debating whether to refill his cup or pour it over his head. "Busy day?"

"Merry!" He brushes a few crumbs from his chest and straightens, eying me warily. "I just stepped out for a minute. You know, your coffee...these pastries...everything's just so irresistible here."

"Why don't I make you another cup to go?" I ask, pointedly. "And maybe another danish?"

"Well, now. That would be mighty sweet of you." He chuckles. "Sweet. Like the pastry, get it?"

"How's my house coming?" I stack his dishes and manage to get a hold of them and the coffee pot before I walk away. "Making progress?"

"Making progress." Bill sighs but obediently follows me towards the counter. "Slowly. Well, it's a big job."

"You said." I clench my jaw but manage a polite smile. "But you are making progress?"

"I've made a start." He is all evasion and I try not to take my frustration out on his order. The last thing I need is for him to add sugary pastry crumbs to every surface of my house, inviting

yet more insects in for a spell. "It'll take a while. You know. It's a
_"

"Big job." I nod. "Well, you'd better keep your strength up
then. Here you go. No charge."

He's so pleased with this that he starts whistling as he makes
his way towards the door and I watch him turn the wrong way
down the high street, heading in the opposite direction from my
house. *He'd better be walking towards his truck, or so help me...*

"Merry!"

I snap to attention at a bright voice and see Jean waving at
me from three people down the queue. Checking Phoebe is on
top of things - she is, and I thank my lucky stars I decided to hire
her - I slide up to say hello.

"I'm glad I caught you, dear." Jean smiles. "I'm running
errands." She brandishes a basket filled with groceries and her
smile fades. "Poor Hannah isn't well at all, so I'm in charge
tonight." She winks. "And you know what that means!"

"No." My hand strays to my earlobe, seeking out the earring
I tug on whenever I get nervous, but my fingers clasp only air. I
frown, trying to remember if I left them on my bedside table in
my rush to get dressed that morning. "What does that mean?"

"All rules are off the table!" She cackles and clutches her
basket a little bit tighter. "I'm making a couple of changes to
the menu. I'm sure Anton won't mind." I think of the grim,
bad-tempered French chef that has made Harmony Inn his home
and wonder if Jean knows something about him I don't.
"Anyway." She shakes her head. "It'll swell the pantry a little bit.
You never can have too much of a good thing." She reaches into
a basket. "Which is why I brought an extra bar of my favorite
honeycomb and almond chocolate. Here! You take it, dear."

"Me?" I hold my hands up to refuse. "Believe me, I have no shortage of sweet treats." We've made it to the front of the queue and I point at the glass pastry case, wincing when I see just how bare it's gotten in the last half-hour. "Excuse me. I'd better get back in the kitchen!"

"I'll leave your chocolate right here, dear!" Jean says, handing it to Phoebe with a smile as she places her order. "And we'll see you for dinner tonight. You're bringing that nice young man of yours, aren't you?"

"Am I?" I hesitate in the doorway. If Rob's coming for dinner at the Harmony Inn tonight it's the first I've heard of it. "Uh...maybe." I glance over my shoulder at the oven and see a batch of cookies I've forgotten about turning from well-done to charcoal and let the door swing closed behind me. I'll call Rob later and ask him about dinner. *Or maybe I won't. If Jean's in charge it'll hardly be Harmony Inn proper.* I smile wickedly to myself, thinking that I'd like my boyfriend to experience Hannah Kincaid in all her glory, which he won't manage to do if she's laid up in bed.

Poor Hannah. I go to work making a fresh batch of cookies I'm determined not to burn this time, and meditatively roll out a larger batch, privately deciding to keep a half-dozen back to take home with me. If she's not feeling well then this might be just the thing to cheer her up, especially if she's going to be dealing with Jean managing the inn without her. If I know anything about Hannah Kincaid it's that she makes micromanaging an art form. She won't voluntarily step down from running the Harmony Inn, and if illness has forced her into bed, she's going to be lying there fretting, not resting. *Maybe I should add a dose of knock-out juice. She's going to need it!*

• • • •

I'M STARTING TO CLOSE down for the day when the door swings open and a familiar male voice reaches my ears.

"Here she is!"

I'm smiling before I even turn around, but the expression freezes on my face when I see my boyfriend has his arm around another woman.

"See? The Jitterbug Junction. Isn't she great? Oh, hey, Merry! We were hoping we'd catch you before you shut up for the day." It's then that I understand the *she* that's so *great* isn't me, but my cafe. "Are we too late for coffee?"

"I'm just closing everything down," I say before Phoebe pops up out of nowhere with her usual absurd need to be helpful.

"But of course we're never going to say no to a friend of the cafe! Latte?" She beams at Rob, then turns an inquisitive look at Chris.

"Make it two. Take out." She eyes me, then shrugs out of Rob's embrace and takes a slow circle of the cafe, which is mercifully empty of customers and looking tidier and cleaner than it has all day. "Well, Merry, this place is just lovely. I'm kind of jealous you get to work here all day!"

"You wouldn't be saying that if you'd had to unclog old coffee grounds from a temperamental machine more than once this week." I continue wiping tables and stacking chairs.

"Let me tell you, old coffee grounds would be the least of my concerns." Chris exchanges a look with Rob and stifles a grin. "Working around animals I usually have to spend my time unclogging other things..."

I frown until my boyfriend's comical face clues me in. *Gross.*

"Well, that's why sensible people choose to work in the hospitality industry, not the veterinary one," Phoebe calls, as she hands two paper cups over and waives off the charge.

"Are you a vet too?" I ask, thinking I don't actually know very much at all about Rob's college friend. There's something so warm and familiar about the way they are together that I feel an unpleasant prickle of jealousy. I turn away, trying to swallow the feeling. I've never been one of those suspicious, clingy girlfriends, but somehow Chris's arrival is making me second-guess everything about my relationship with Rob. He seems to sense something's wrong because I feel him come up behind me and drop a kiss on the top of my head. I lean into him and feel my silly burst of jealousy fade as swiftly as it had appeared.

"Chris works with animals."

"Ha!"

I feel the low rumble of laughter in Rob's chest and lean away from him, trying to figure out what is so funny, but he and Chris have some kind of inside joke they don't feel like sharing. My good mood sours and even Rob swinging into helpful-boyfriend mode, packing down the cafe in half the time I would have taken, isn't enough to fully restore it.

"Well, I'd better get home to my furry little houseguest." Phoebe winks at me. I know she's done me a favor by taking in Snuffy for a few days but honestly, she seems to be enjoying it almost as much as he is. I make a mental note to treat her to something special as a thank you once this week is over and then recall just how long Bill the Bug Guy lingered over his break here today. *Maybe* week *is a little optimistic.* I sigh, wondering how long I'm going to be living out of a suitcase and dealing with Harmony Inn dynamics, and that's when I remember Jean's comment from earlier.

"Oh, I think you've been invited to dinner at the inn tonight," I say to Rob, as he and Chris head to the door and allow me and Phoebe to switch off the lights and lock up.

"He certainly has!" Chris nudges him with her elbow. "I invited him!"

"You did?" My voice sounds sharper than I mean it to and I try to soften it with a smile that's only partly successful.

"Once I heard about you having to vacate your home because of termites I thought you might want a little familiarity." She winks at me. "Plus, I think you and I could do with adding a little more normal to that table. Tip the balance in our favor."

"Ha!" There's that look again, the shared joke between them that I'm not part of. Rob catches my expression and misreads it. "Unless you don't want me there?" He offers me his hand and I reluctantly take it. "I'm perfectly happy with ramen noodles on the sofa if you'd rather have Chris and the Harmony Inn Oddities all to yourself." There's something gently teasing about his tone of voice and I can't help but smile.

"You make them sound like a folk band." I hum a little ditty. "The Harmony Inn Oddities."

"Don't give Jean any ideas." Chris shudders. "Ever since Hannah fell ill today, Jean's been in full dictator mode. I wouldn't be surprised to find she's redecorated and doubled the price on every room in the place." She winces. "When the cat's away..."

"But the cat isn't away! Hannah's just under the weather, I heard."

"Oh, she is. She took a funny turn at breakfast." Chris looks at me. "After you left. She stood up to clear the table and nearly fainted. That was when Jean chased her away to bed and dispatched that mousy little maid up with a fresh pot of tea. Wouldn't even trust her or Anton to make it, she did it all herself." Chris pulls a face. "If you ask me, control issues run high in that family."

"They're cousins, aren't they?" Rob asks, as we reach the small parking bay where my car is waiting for me. I see his parked one bay over and he hesitates before fishing out his keys and tossing them to Chris. "Why don't you go on ahead?"

"Alright, alright!" Chris laughs. "You two want some alone time. You don't need to tell me twice!"

"We'll be right behind you!" I say, feeling heat pool in my cheeks and wondering why I feel like a teenager again when I'm comfortably into my thirties.

"Sure will," Rob agrees. "I don't want to miss a single beat of the Harmony Inn Oddities." He pauses. "And you can let me know what's different now Jean is in charge."

Chapter Four

Dinner at the inn does not disappoint. Having made it through breakfast I was expecting more of the same, but with Hannah absent and with Jean in charge, more than a few things seem different.

"And what do you do, Rob?" Dan asks, chipping in with a question the instant his wife pauses for breath.

"I'm a vet." Rob straightens his cutlery. "Animals, not military."

"Oh, how lovely! We love animals, don't we, Dan?" Sally beams at the whole table. "We have cats. Or rather, we did have cats. We had to give them up when - "

"I'm allergic," Dan says, with a sharp look at his wife. Sally's smile dims for all of a minute, but she is soon her cheery self again.

"And how was your day, Merry? Was the cafe busy? We meant to pop down and see you but time just escaped us. Perhaps tomorrow!"

"You'd be more than welcome," I say, trying to sound more enthusiastic than I feel. Dan and Sally are a perfectly lovely couple but there's something a little off about them.

"We want to compare it now to how it was when Maggie was at the helm." Dan winks at me, then lets out a booming laugh. "See which one of you does it better."

"That'd be Merry," Rob says, loyally. He slides an arm around the back of my chair. "You've only had the running of the place for a few months but you've certainly made it your own."

"I've been lucky. Maggie had made such a success of it to start with. And people in Silver Brook have generously kept coming."

"They don't have much choice," Edgar pipes up from his corner of the table. He's poring over yet another book, making furious notes on his phone as he reads. I hadn't realized he'd even been aware there were other people in the room, let alone listening to our conversation. "As I said at breakfast, yours is the only cafe in town." He slides his glasses further up his nose. "You could serve terrible coffee and stale cakes and people would still buy from you."

My mouth falls open and I'm so stunned I'm not quite sure how to respond. Fortunately, I don't have to. Chris does it for me.

"Well, I can confirm Merry's coffee certainly isn't terrible. And I haven't had a chance to try her baking yet but I'm pretty sure that's stellar too. Isn't that right, Rob?"

My boyfriend smiles self-deprecatingly and pats his midsection.

"I'm close to busting through my jeans because I can't say no to trying every new snack she comes up with."

"It's important to remember moderation where sweets are concerned," Edgar begins again, and I can feel tension settle over the table which is broken when the door opens and Delphine scuttles inside, carrying a heavy platter of chicken roast that she struggles to settle safely in the middle of the large table.

"Dinner is served!" Jean calls as she follows her into the room and beams at us. "Or it will be when the rest of the dishes arrive." She frowns. "Go on, Delphine. Hurry up or the meat will be cold before the sides are even here. Anton has everything plated up and ready in the kitchen so you don't even need to speak to him if you don't want to. I'm sure you won't want to feel his wrath if you ruin this wonderful meal he spent all day slaving over for us." She waits until the maid obediently, silently scurries away again then turns to us, awkwardly wrenching her smile back into place. "You know what French chefs are like. Very tempestuous, but they do cook divinely." She peers hungrily at the roast. "I certainly think we'll all eat well today."

"Shall I make a plate up for Hannah?" Chris asks, picking up her plate and leaning forward to spear a particularly juicy piece of chicken.

"No!" Jean's response is so sharp that I jump, and I see Sally clutch her heart as if she, too, was caught off-guard. "You don't need to worry about my cousin." Jean chuckles, and I feel the last of the tension lift. "I've got a nice tray of tea and toast made just the way she likes it in the kitchen. I'll have Delphine run up with it once she finishes in here." She pauses, then disappears back out of the room and we hear her loudly reprimanding the maid for her slowness. I glance at Rob but he's exchanging a wary look with Chris and I try not to feel slighted. I turn instead to Sally and ask what she and Dan found to occupy them today, and whether they had enjoyed themselves.

"Oh, very much!" Sally sighs, contentedly. "We do love our yearly visits to Silver Brook. We have a whole agenda we have to follow every time we're here, don't we darling?"

"We certainly do, darling." Dan takes a long sip of his water and I wonder if he is quite as excited about this agenda as his wife seems to be.

"First of all, we went to Milford Point. It's not far from here and there's an old woodland path that leads to the clearing. It starts just near the inn and winds its way uphill. Very pretty."

"You know that's where the two founding families had a showdown that led to the deaths of twenty people?" Edgar observes, pausing to turn a page. "And six cows?"

"What?"

"Well, I certainly wasn't aware of that!" Sally giggles, uncomfortably. "I'm not sure I would have found it such a romantic spot if I'd known I was standing on a literal graveyard!"

"They didn't bury them there," Edgar begins, and I can sense our dining table conversation is about to take a turn for the macabre when a flurry of angry words comes from the corridor before the door swings open again and a large brute of a man with an undersized chef's hat balanced on his bald, tattooed head, bursts into the room.

"Et voila!" He slams down a container of green beans with a flourish and straightens, adjusting his hat and surveying us with a look that can only really be described as menacing. "Bon appetit!"

We all stare up at him in silence for a moment until a small cough makes him realize that Delphine has sidled in after him, clutching a tray with two other dishes that need adding to the table. With a bit of rearranging everything is soon displayed to the best advantage and both Delphine and Anton retreat from view.

"Well, this all looks delicious," Dan begins, with manful enthusiasm. "I suppose we ought to wait for Jean to come back?"

Rob pauses with his plate halfway towards the chicken, then lowers it back to the table with a wry smile.

We aren't waiting long before we hear another flurry of angry instructions from Jean who bursts back into the dining room looking flustered and irritable. She pats her gray hair into place and smiles at us.

"Well, don't stand on ceremony, everybody. Dig in!"

· · · ·

"THAT WAS DELICIOUS, Ms. Montrose!" Rob declares, as he finishes his last bite of dessert - an elegant fruit pavlova dripping with cream. "I think I should come to eat here every night!"

"Just Jean, dear. And you'd be most welcome!" Jean twinkles at him, then at me. "Especially as long as Merry is staying with us."

"Yes, the food is one of the best parts of staying here at the Harmony Inn," Dan says with a contented yawn. "Do pass on our compliments to the chef, won't you?"

"C'etait une tuerie," Edgar remarks, in the stiffest french accent I've ever heard. He must sense our collective mystification because he looks up - still reading, even while eating - and blinks at us. "He's a French chef, isn't he?"

"He is!" Jean glares at the door and then begins stacking our plates. "And he will be delighted to hear that you all enjoyed your meals. *Une tuerie.*" She tries Edgar's phrase out, pursing her lips around the unfamiliar words. "Perhaps I'll send him back in to collect the rest of the dishes and you can tell him that yourself, dear." She glances back towards the door. "I can't think where Delphine has got to. She ought to be doing this."

"I can go look for her," Chris offers. "Let me take those."

"Let me." I jump up, and as I'm closer to Jean it's me who wins this particular battle. My arms sag under the weight of the plates but I'm determined to be useful - and I'm more than a little eager to avoid another showdown between Jean and poor Delphine. "Which way is the kitchen?" Jean directs me and I hurry down the corridor and into the crowded, messy kitchen which for a moment seems deserted.

"No, you listen to me!"

I flinch, then see the back of Chef Anton's shoulder. He's standing half inside what looks like a pantry with his back to me and he's in the middle of a fraught, angry conversation. Everyone's nerves seem to be frazzled today, and that's when it hits me that not only is our French chef speaking English, but he is doing so without any trace of an accent. I'm mystified and take a step closer, curiosity outweighing the bad manners of listening in on a stranger's conversation. Before I can move very far, though, I'm stopped in my tracks by the sound of a scream from overhead. Not just any scream. Even at a distance, I recognize that strangled voice. *Hannah!*

Chapter Five

The scream might have been Hannah Kincaid's but the disaster that caused it hadn't happened to her at all.

"Delly! Delphine! Oh, dear!"

I bolt out of the kitchen and can sense Anton right on my heels, but there's a collision in the hallway with several other people who react the same as us.

"Allow me!" Jean declares, wrenching through the crush of people and clambering upstairs. She looks a little white-faced and anxious, and something about her cousin's scream makes my stomach turn over in an eerily familiar way. I meet Rob's gaze and see my suspicions reflected in his pale, serious face.

"Can I help at all, Ms. Montrose?" he asks, slipping into professional mode. He might not be a medical doctor - not for humans, anyway - but that doesn't mean he isn't a good man to have around in a crisis.

"Yes, is something the matter? Hannah? Are you alright?"

Chris pushes upstairs behind Rob - ahead of me - and despite my eagerness to follow I decide I can be more useful in directing the other anxious people that surround me.

"Come on." I inject my voice with a little forced brightness. "Let's go into the sitting room, shall we? I'm sure whatever's happened up there Hannah won't want an audience."

The assembled crowd has only just begun to disperse when a choked shout echoes out of the room, pinning us all in place.

"She's dead!"

Who's dead? Instantly I turn around, my hand still on the rail when Rob barrels downstairs towards me, his phone pressed against his ear.

"Yes, an ambulance. The Harmony Inn, in Silver Brook..." He presses a hand gently to my cheek as he passes me which is the only clue he's seen me at all. His features are pinched and anxious, and I follow him almost without meaning to.

"What happened?" I ask, as he pauses in his words and holds the phone away from his ear for a moment. "They're sending an ambulance?"

Rob nods, peering over my shoulder to check I haven't been followed. He takes me by the arm and steers me around the side of the inn to a comfortable area of the sheltered porch that has a swing seat and a table set for backgammon that one of the other guests is halfway through playing. I blink, wondering why at a time of crisis like this I even notice a thing like that.

"I don't want you to panic," Rob says, in a low voice. "But it looks like she's been poisoned."

"Who? Hannah?" My hand flies to my mouth and I think of how she took to her bed earlier today.

Rob shakes his head, his lips drawn in a tight line.

"No. She's ok. Physically, she's fine. It's Delly."

My mind goes blank, trying to place who on earth *Delly* is.

"The maid. Delphine."

"Oh no!" I sag and Rob steers me towards the porch swing, settling me into it before perching next to me. "What happened?"

Rob holds the phone back towards his ear for a moment, listening to something the medics on the other side are saying, before nodding.

"Thank you," he says. "I'll be out front so I can greet them when they get here." He ends the call and drops the phone onto the seat between us. "I don't know what happened," he confesses, drawing a weary breath. "When I got there it was too late. She was gone." He rakes a hand through his hair. "Chris is trying to get some details out of Hannah, but she's so shaken..."

"But Delphine was just fine a few minutes ago!" I frown, trying to remember just how many minutes have elapsed since I last saw the quiet mouse of a maid. "Are you sure she was poisoned?"

Rob nods, hesitating as if he's unsure whether to tell me something or not. I fix him with a look and eventually he relents.

"I think - I don't know - I think I've seen something like it before." A muscle in his jaw twitches. "In animals."

My eyes widen but I don't say anything, knowing silence is sometimes better than questions in getting someone cagey to open up. Rob starts telling me an old vet school story about a wave of poisonings affecting local cats that were eventually traced to one particular person. His gaze travels up and I can see from the way his features pinch that he's remembering what he just saw in Hannah's room.

"We should call the police." I reach for his phone, expecting him to stop me but he leans back in the swing, losing all his fight. He doesn't say a word as I place a call with the police station, asking expressly for Police Chief Trainor. He and I have had our differences in the past, and I'd be lying if I didn't admit I'd rather call Kate, my best friend and the hardest-working police deputy in Silver Brook. *But Kate's out of town, and this isn't the time to be choosy.* If Rob's hunch is right - and I've no reason to believe it isn't - we've got a poisoner in our midst.

I shiver and Rob automatically reaches for me, pulling me against him. I'm not sure which of us needs the embrace more. We wait like that, saying nothing until the sound of sirens breaks the tension.

"Come on," I say, standing and pulling him up alongside me. I shoot him a wary, sad smile and remind him this isn't the first time we've beaten the police to a crime scene.

• • • •

"MS. GRAY."

Police Chief Trainor doesn't actually roll his eyes when he sees me standing with the crowd of other guests in the Harmony Inn sitting room, but I can hear the vague note of irritation in his voice that yet again he's been called to investigate a murder and yet again I'm one of the first people he sees on the scene.

"Oh, Jim, I'm so glad you're here!" Jean sniffs, stepping in front of me to greet the police chief like he's an old friend. Which I guess, to her, he is.

"Ms. Montrose." He tips his head, not quite a bow, but she waves away any hint of formality by clutching his arm. He awkwardly steers her towards a chair, pointedly clearing his throat when Edgar, who has taken up residence in the most comfortable of the living room's armchairs, doesn't immediately move.

"You'll want to interview all of us, won't you?" Edgar asks, glancing at his watch. "Not that any of us have anything helpful to offer. We've all just been here." He gestures around the room and I see Trainor's brow crease in a frown as he counts us and notices someone missing.

"Hannah is upstairs," I offer before he can ask. "With -"

"The deceased?"

I shake my head.

"With Chris - Christine Watson, one of the other guests here. And with Rob."

"Christine Watson?" Trainor's features rearrange themselves into something marginally less irritated and I begin to wonder why Chris's presence here is less of an annoyance than mine. And just how come Chief Trainor knows who she is.

"The EMTs took the -" I stop myself before referring to *the deceased* or *the body* and remind myself that only an hour ago she was a living, breathing person. "They took Delphine to the hospital."

"The hospital?" Trainor looks at Edgar for confirmation. "I thought she died?"

"She did." He nods. "Probably they'll want to do some tests to figure out what killed her. Whether it was some kind of poison or an illness. And they'll want to rule out something contagious." Dan and Sally pointedly shuffle a few steps away from Edgar when he makes this suggestion and I turn back to Trainor, wanting a break from my fellow guests for a few minutes.

"I'll show you where Hannah's room is." I glance down at Jean to check she's ok with me taking charge. She seems shaken, but otherwise alright, and she struggles to her feet until I lay a hand on her shoulder. "You stay here, Jean," I say, as gently as I can. "I'll show Chief Trainor where he needs to go."

"Yes, stay here," the police chief says, with a wary look around the room. "Everyone stay here, and I'll be right back to take your statements once I've seen - ah - once I've spoken to the others."

I hear a flurry of muttered complaints from Edgar, Dan, and Sally and hurry out of the room. The sooner Trainor starts taking statements, the sooner all of us can go to our own rooms. I stifle a yawn, wondering just how much sleep I'll manage to get tonight. I may have stumbled over more than my fair share of murders, but I'm not sure I want to spend the night in the same building where one just took place.

Chapter Six

Neither, it turns out, does Hannah. She vacates her room as soon as the EMTs move in, and has co-opted the only other empty room in the inn, perching primly on the edge of an overstuffed quilt and eyeing the door from behind a huge lace-trimmed handkerchief she keeps pinned to her nose.

"You'll have to forgive me, James," she says, addressing the police chief by his first name as if he's still a child and not a middle-aged man. "It's not every day a young woman drops dead right in front of you." She sniffs theatrically and looks reproachfully in my direction. "And when the house is full of guests, too!"

"That can't be helped," Chief Trainor says philosophically. He takes a step forward, hesitates, and then settles his considerable bulk next to Hannah on the bed. "Why don't you tell me everything you can remember?" He catches her sharp look and offers a qualifier. "About this evening. About - what was the young girl's name? Delphine?"

"Delly." Hannah nods. "Such a sweet girl." She gives another theatrical sniff and Chief Trainor braces for tears that don't come. He looks relieved when Hannah masters herself and turns to him, almost businesslike. "So what do you want to know? She came in to check on me and brought me a cup of tea made just the way I like." She purses her lips. "Never can trust Anton with that. Anyway, I didn't quite feel like drinking it, so I left it to one side and asked her to sit down for a few minutes and talk to me. I'm sure you can't imagine, James, how lonely it gets, being cooped up in one's room all day."

"Had you been cooped up in here - I mean, in there. Have you been in your room all day?"

"Since breakfast. I took a little turn." Hannah blushes. "I've been feeling so run down lately. I'm sure it's just a little cold but I can't seem to shake it, and with Jean here..." She frowns. "Well, she insisted on me spending the day in bed. Said she could handle everything just fine without me." Her lips quirk in annoyance.

"That's kind of her," Chief Trainor jumps in, re-directing Hannah's irritation with her cousin. "I'm sure that extra rest did you the world of good. So this evening, Delphine came and sat with you for a little while. Then what?"

"Well, she was telling me this long, convoluted story about Tim - that's her beau." Hannah's gaze dances towards me, and Chief Trainor seems surprised to notice I'm still standing in the doorway, listening to every word Hannah says. I back away, but not before I hear Hannah start to speak again.

"I don't suppose they use the word *beau* these days, but that's what this young man is. Or was." She pauses, and I hear the effort it costs her to keep speaking. "She was a little upset. They'd argued, you see, and so I told her to drink my tea. I always have plenty of sugar, and the sweetness is good for - for shock."

"She drank your tea?"

I freeze in the doorway. This is the first I've heard about this. Rob thought Delphine must have ingested something, but he wasn't sure what.

"Drank it right down." Hannah nods. "Then she went ever so pale, and as she stood to leave the room she collapsed and then - and then..." She trails off, sniffing noisily into her handkerchief while Chief Trainor awkwardly tries to comfort her.

I continue to creep away, but I haven't made it more than a couple of steps before the police chief's voice calls after me.

"Merry? If you're going to lurk in the doorway, at least make yourself useful. Why don't you ask your boyfriend to come and talk to me, and Ms. Watson too? I want to know what they can add to Hannah's story."

• • • •

"HI, JIM. GOOD TO SEE you."

Chris strolls into the room already on first-name terms with Chief Trainor and I fight the urge to stare.

"Christine! I thought that was you." Chief Trainor straightens and sucks in his gut a little, forcing his features into the kind of smile he's never bothered using around me. I sour and Rob notices, shooting me a questioning look, but I wave him off.

"Chief Trainor is taking statements," I say. "He wanted to start with you two, as you found - you were…"

"I gather you were both first on the scene." Chief Trainor lays a comforting hand on Hannah's shoulder. "And Ms. Kincaid has told me everything she remembers."

"Do you want to stay here, Hannah?" I ask, thinking that I've never seen her look so frail before. "Why don't you come down to the kitchen with me and we'll see if we can persuade Anton to fix us something to eat."

"Can't let you do that, I'm afraid!" Chief Trainor booms. He taps his notebook with the nib of his pen. "Haven't questioned him yet." His eyes narrow as he looks at me. "Or you."

"We'll stay here, then." I fold my arms and meet Trainor's gaze. I know he's not my biggest fan, and after the stories I've heard from Kate about what he's like to work with - not to mention witnessing his approach to crime-solving the last few times we've been forced to interact - I can say the feeling is mutual.

"Not so fast." Trainor looks like he's doing a particularly complicated math problem in his head. "You stay." He points me to a chair next to Hannah, then turns to Rob and Chris. "We'll go back to the - uh - other room." He raises his eyebrows and I guess that it's taken all of his energy not to call Hannah Kincaid's bedroom a crime scene. "I need to make some observations, anyway."

I stifle a laugh, turning it vaguely into a cough, and sit down next to Hannah, who looks so pale and frail, so unlike her usual self, that I reach for her hand. We sit in silence until the other three leave us, closing the door behind them with a sharp click.

"Don't worry," I promise her, with more confidence than I feel. "Chief Trainor will get to the bottom of this."

"I hope so." Hannah sighs, tiredly, then reaches into the pocket of her robe for her handkerchief. Pulling it out brings something else along with it and something sparkling and silver drops onto the floor. I instinctively reach for it.

"Oh, is that yours, dear?" Hannah blows her nose, then reaches back into her pocket. "Here's the other one." She hands me the second of my two missing earrings. "I found them on the floor in my room of all places!" She shakes her head. "Can't imagine what they were doing there. Anyway, I thought I recognized them. I'm glad to be able to return them." Her voice wobbles and I sense another wave of tears coming. "It's nice for something to be resolved for good on this awful night."

I'm still too numb to say much. I hold my missing earrings flat in the palm of my hand, watching as the glass beads sparkle in the light. *I found them on the floor in my room*. What had they been doing in Hannah's room? I certainly hadn't dropped them there. I'd left them carefully on my bedside table - exactly where I hadn't found them this morning. *So how did they end up in the room where a murder just happened?*

Chapter Seven

The Harmony Inn feels like a ghost town when I tiptoe through it the next morning. After a sleepless night, I eventually decide to get up early and go to work. I don't suppose anybody will feel like sitting around the dining table eating breakfast this morning, and I know an extra hour to myself in the sanctuary of the Jitterbug Junction will help soothe my frazzled nerves.

I'm just waking up the coffee machine for my first cup when I get a text from Rob asking how I am and whether I want to meet him for breakfast. I hit reply so fast that I'm fairly sure autocorrect makes most of my answer unreadable. He figures it out, though, sending me back a coffee cup emoji and a question mark. I send him a thumbs-up and get out another clean mug. I'm just pouring his coffee out when I see his shadowy figure approach the cafe's locked front door and I dart out to let him inside.

"Hi." My smile dims when I notice how tired he looks. "Did you sleep at all last night?"

"Did you?" He runs his thumb over the bags under my eyes and presses his forehead against mine. "How was it?"

"Quiet." We walk back up to the counter and I pass him one of the lattes I've made us. "Although I hope you won't think any less of me if I admit to barricading myself into my room all night. Those single-traveler hotel safety influencers have nothing on my set-up."

"Good." Rob pulls out a stool and sits down. "And did you eat anything?"

"Why do you think I came into work so early?" I disappear into the kitchen and emerge with a sealed tupperware box. "How do stale croissants sound?"

"Like the perfect breakfast."

I put the box down between the two of us and we each take one, talking as we eat.

"So what do you think?" Rob glances at me.

"About?" I take a dainty bite of my croissant and still manage to shower myself with crumbs. Rolling my eyes, I brush away the worst of them and reach for my coffee. "I think I'm going to need to sweep the floor again before we open up."

"I'll help you." Rob adds his crumbs to the mix. "But I was asking about last night. The murder. What do you think?"

"I think it's a tragedy." I eye him. "Are we sure it's a murder?"

"Are we sure it isn't?" He finishes his croissant and turns in his seat to meet my gaze. "Come on, Merry. I know you. You must have some idea who's behind this. Either that or you're itching to find out. So..."

"I'm leaving it to the police," I say, sweetly, which is apparently unconvincing because my boyfriend laughs and reaches for another pastry. "Oh, alright. I have no idea yet, but..." I finger my earrings and decide it's a strange enough detail that I might as well share it. "Hannah said she found my earrings in her room."

"Those earrings?"

I nod.

"But I've never been in her room. I left them on my bedside table the other night and when I woke up they were gone."

Rob's eyebrows lift, and his interest spurs me on.

"There's something else, too. Delphine and Jean were rowing a lot last night. About silly stuff. She was taking too long to serve the dinner, that sort of thing. But Hannah made some comment the other day about how Delphine was threatening her."

"Sounds like it's the other way around. Hannah takes business at the Harmony Inn pretty seriously. If Delphine isn't doing her job - and if she's helping herself to other people's belongings..." He nods at my earrings. "Maybe Delphine's death will solve a problem or two for the Kincaid-Montroses." Rob jokes, but it doesn't seem so funny after everything that's happened.

"You don't think Hannah could be responsible, do you? It was her tea Delphine drank, after all." I think back over how tightly she held my hand last night, and how often she pressed her lace handkerchief to her eyes. For someone usually so strict and aloof, she did seem very emotional. *Yes,* I tell myself. *Because she just saw somebody die.* Another thought occurs to me and I voice it. "Maybe someone was trying to poison Hannah."

"Or maybe Hannah wanted it to look like that." Rob and I hold each other's gaze for a moment before shaking our heads and turning back to our breakfasts.

"Anything's possible," he says, after a long moment's pause. "But I think you should be careful if you're going to stay at the inn. You don't actually know any of the people there."

"Neither do you," I point out. I'm grateful that he cares, but I'm still stubbornly clinging to my independence. "Apart from Chris."

"Chris can take care of herself."

"And I can't?" My voice is a little sharper than I mean it to be and Rob looks hurt. I ought to backtrack, but something keeps me moving forward. "I've witnessed more than my fair share of murders recently, you know, and lived to tell the tale."

"Only just," Rob reminds me. "And what is so wrong about me wanting to keep you safe?"

"Nothing," I concede at last. "But it's not necessary. I'm fine." I hope my words sound more convincing to him than they do to me. "I'm going to be fine." I hop off my stool and start gathering up the last of the leftover pastries and our empty coffee mugs. "But I'm never going to get this place open on time if I don't start now. I gave Phoebe the morning off, so it's all on me today."

Rob watches me work, meditatively chewing on the last bite of his croissant. He seems to come to a decision because he gets slowly to his feet and follows me into the kitchen.

"I'm not due into work for a few hours yet. I could stick around and give you a hand if you want." He seems to pre-empt my protest because he's already reaching for an apron when I turn around. "Just to keep the cafe ticking over. When it comes to dealing with murderers, I know, you can handle yourself."

He's teasing me, and I deserve worse, but I can't help but feel a tiny shudder of nerves. If there really is a murderer on the loose at the Harmony Inn, I'm not the only one who might be in danger. *Which is all the more reason to figure out who they are quickly, before anyone else gets hurt.*

· · · ·

"I'VE BEEN WANTING AN excuse to play with this coffee machine." Rob grins at me, wiggling his fingers in feigned excitement. "Where do we start? Double-shot, extra foam, cappuccino?"

"You can run the register," I say, pointing him toward the Jitterbug Junction's old-school manual cash register. "Key in the prices, hit the button, and give people their change." I locate my one nod to modernity, a nondescript silver tablet. "Or get them to point their card, phone, smartwatch, whatever they want to use at this little piece of black magic."

"Not a fan of technology, are you, babe?"

"I am when it works." I eye the coffee machine, which is temperamental at the best of times. "Right. We've restocked the pastries and cakes, you know how to take payments, and I can handle drinks. I think we're ready to open and it's still only..." I glance at my watch, then let out a yelp. "Time we got down to business." I dash across the cafe, straightening tables and chairs as I go and wrench open the door, turning the sign to a cheerful we-are-open. To my relief, there isn't a crowd of eager customers waiting for their first coffee of the day. There are two, and my heart sinks as I recognize them.

"Meredith! Good morning! See, darling, I told you we were just early!"

"You did, darling, you did." Dan leans past me to peer into the cafe. "Gosh, it looks a lot bigger when you have no customers, doesn't it?"

"You've timed it just right," I say, through a pained smile. "You're my first two of the day."

"Unless you count me!" Rob calls from his spot behind the cash register. "What can we get for you two lovebirds?"

"Takes one to know one!" Sally coos, letting go of her husband and tottering towards the counter with her wide eyes fixed on the pastry case. "Oh, those cakes look divine! We haven't had breakfast yet." Her gaze meets mine as I come to join Rob, ready to make whatever drinks they request. "It didn't feel right to stay and eat at the inn. Not after -" Her voice drops to a stage whisper. "What happened."

"I'm not sure I'll ever want to eat there again," Dan says, in an incongruously chipper tone. "Knowing there's a poisoner on the loose does tend to do a number on one's appetite. Ooh! Caramel slices!"

I exchange a look with Rob, who's trying hard not to laugh, and I begin to think that maybe today won't be so bad after all.

"You find us a table, darling," Sally says, reaching into her purse for some money. "I'll order. Two coffees, a caramel slice, and a banana-nut muffin, please." She beams as Rob carefully jabs at the cash register and I hurry to make up their drinks. "It's so lovely to see you two working here together! I didn't know you were co-owners."

"We're not!" I say, hurriedly.

"I'm just making up the numbers for an hour or two." Rob frowns at the cash register, which seems to have frozen, and I lean over him to thump the button that releases the cash drawer. "Helping out, you know." Rob grins and hands Sally her change.

"Well, I think that's wonderful!" Sally sighs, then looks mischievously around the empty cafe. "And as long as you don't have any other customers to focus on, maybe you'll join Dan and me for breakfast. You can tell us all about how you two met!"

I glance at Rob, who clearly finds Dan and Sally's schtick more amusing and endearing than I do.

"We'd love to," he says, sliding an arm around my shoulders and steering me towards their table with a grin.

Chapter Eight

If there's one thing to be grateful for running a cafe, it's easy access to an endless supply of caffeine. I pour myself yet another cup of coffee and take a stealthy sip during a break in my lunchtime queue of customers and hope I don't look as tired as I feel.

"What's wrong?" Phoebe asks, with a friendly smile. "Aren't the beds at the Harmony Inn comfortable?"

Something in my expression gives the game away and Phoebe's smile falls.

"Oh no! What happened?"

I shake my head, glancing around to make sure we aren't going to be overheard. The Jitterbug is relatively quiet for the time of day, so I figure if ever there's a time to fill Phoebe in on what happened last night without becoming a source of Silver Brook gossip, it's now. Taking another fortifying sip of coffee I explain about the unfortunate happenings at the inn and tell her the reason I can't stop yawning today is because I spent most of last night waiting to give my statement to Police Chief Trainor, along with the rest of the inn's guests.

"You're kidding!" Phoebe's eyes are as wide as saucers. "And you think the maid was murdered?"

"It looks like it." I shudder and put down my cup before I spill what's left of my coffee all over myself. Remembering we still aren't one hundred percent sure of the source of the poisoning has done a number on my appetite, as well. My stomach churns uncomfortably and I swallow, making a mental note to eat here before I go back to the inn tonight. I wonder if it would be worth taking food back with me because I doubt Anton is going to be allowed free rein of the kitchen until they can be sure he isn't involved...

"What's wrong? You've gone green." Phoebe frowns at me, eyeing my coffee cup warily.

"Just thinking about Delphine," I admit, with a faint smile. "I didn't know her very well - or at all, really - but to think that someone wanted her dead like that..."

"I don't know," Phoebe muses, as she bends into the glass-fronted display cabinet that houses an array of tasty treats and baked goods. "It might not be about her personally."

"What do you mean?"

Phoebe doesn't answer me at first and I'm about to ask my question a second time when she finally backs out of the cupboard and shoots me a look.

"Maybe it's to do with her job."

"She was a maid." I'm non-plussed. "What's so very dangerous about that?"

"Maids learn things," Phoebe points out. "Maybe she witnessed something. Maybe she discovered something while she was tidying up about one of the other guests - oh, good morning, Mr Simms! Your usual?" She jumps from whispering to me to greeting one of our regulars with a bright, cheery smile, and I step out of her way, grateful I can let most of the morning's work fall on her shoulders. I'm too nervy to deal with customers, and too nauseous to be much use in the kitchen. I grab a damp cloth and set to work clearing tables, grateful for something to occupy my hands while my mind turns over the chain of thoughts Phoebe has just sparked. *Maybe she discovered something about one of the other guests...* That would fit with

Trainor's line of questioning. I think back over the previous evening's interviews, trying to determine which of my fellow guests he spent more time with. Dan and Sally were only in there for a few minutes, even though there were two of them. And Edgar was quickly dismissed - although that, I think, is more because he began to get under Chief Trainor's skin by offering his suggestions on how best to run an investigation. I bite my lip, thinking about how my previous involvement in more than one murder in Silver Brook has put me on the police chief's list of people he'd rather not have to deal with.

The Jitterbug door swings open and I sense a familiar gait, but when I look up it isn't who I think it is. Jean isn't bustling into the cafe with an inquiring look on her face. Hannah is.

"Meredith!" She beckons me over to join her, and I leave my tray of dirty cups and saucers where it sits, wiping my hands absent-mindedly on my apron and hurrying over to the corner booth she's awkwardly sliding into.

"Hannah, what can I get you? How are you holding up?"

"About as well as you'd think when a murder happened under my roof!" She eyes me sternly as if she thinks I had something to do with it. "I just couldn't stay there anymore. I needed to get some fresh air, and to think." She shakes her bag at me and it rattles, and when I frown she sighs, then reaches inside, pulling out a jumble of thread and quilt pieces. "I am going to sit here and work my stitches until I figure out just who is going around attacking my staff!"

"Surely you can leave that to Chief Trainor to sort out," I suggest, eyeing the needle she violently begins stabbing into her fabric. "After all, I don't think anything else will happen right away, not with Delphine -"

"That's where you're wrong." Hannah's eyes gleam. "And that's exactly why I couldn't stay there alone all day. Not after what happened to Anton!"

• • • •

"THE POLICE CAN'T THINK he has something to do with it!"

Even as I saying this I wonder why I'm questioning it. Of course the police think he has something to do with it. It's a natural assumption if someone has been poisoned to blame the chef. My stomach turns over when I remember the peculiar behavior I witnessed in the kitchen last night before Delphine died and I wonder if I should mention it.

"Well of course they think that!" Hannah is tearful, and her response makes me shut my mouth before I say anything that might upset her more. "Unless they think I had something to do with it." She pauses. "I didn't! And anyway, the tea and toast Delphine brought upstairs was for me. And why on earth would Anton want to hurt me?"

I bite my lip, thinking that the quick pivot from Anton *could never hurt anyone* to Anton *would never hurt me* probably wouldn't help his case. Hannah's thoughts are so jumbled it takes me a moment to get them straight in my mind and I watch as she methodically pieces a section of her quilt, wondering how she can keep her stitches so neat when her brain is jumping in seven different directions at once.

"Where is Anton now?" I ask, thinking I'd like to question him a little myself if I can get to him without Chief Trainor around to cramp my style.

"He's at home." Hannah's needles click furiously. "Barricaded in the kitchen and complaining about not being able to do his job." She shakes her head. "I don't know what we're going to feed everyone tonight. That's if - if people even want to eat! I've already had guests talking about checking out early."

"Who?" This is something worth pursuing. Sure, guests might be cutting their stays short because they don't want to be caught up in a murder, but they might also want to get out before their crimes catch up to them. I run through the guests in my head, trying to guess if any of them had a reason to want to hurt Delphine. *Or Hannah*, I think. *If it was her drink that was poisoned.*

"Well, Dan and Sally! They're checking out today."

"But wasn't their visit coming to an end anyway?" I think back to the celebratory dinner we had last night before disaster struck. "They were getting ready to go home."

"I suppose." Hannah frowns, and it seems like my attempt to cheer her up has had the opposite effect. "But then there are future guests who might cancel their visit if they find out about this. You know, the Harmony Inn has a reputation to uphold."

I hear a loud, pointed sniff and turn in the direction of Phoebe. She gives me a look and I'm reminded of what she confided in me before about Harmony Inn's questionable history.

"I'm sure everything will all turn out ok." I pat Hannah gently on the arm. "Look at Peter's bookstore." There had been an unfortunate death connected to a book launch held at the popular high-street store that had somehow become the making of the place. Even now crime enthusiasts and readers travel from miles around to visit his store. "His business has gone from strength to strength since...what happened." I drop my voice to a whisper, not wanting to carry as far as Phoebe's ears. That murder had been the reason she stayed in Silver Brook and I'm sure she doesn't need reminding of it now.

"But I don't want the first thing people think of when they hear *Harmony Inn* to be...murder. It was bad enough when they used to think of -" She stops suddenly, glancing at me and it takes effort to keep my expression neutral. "Never mind."

The door to the Jitterbug swings open and Jean bursts through it, scanning the room before her gaze comes to settle on us.

"Hannah! There you are." She makes her way over to join us, staggering under the weight of several heavy bags. "I told you if you weren't well enough to come into town I could run all the errands."

"I'm fine." Hannah glares at her cousin. "Just taking a few moments to catch up with Meredith here."

Jean shoots me a look that is pure eloquence and I jump out of my seat to attention.

"Would you both like something to eat or drink? Here, Jean, sit for a minute."

"Thank you, no." Jean draws in a breath, then seems to thaw. "One of us should be on hand at the inn to keep business ticking over. It's a good job I'm here to help out, isn't it, Hannah? As I've been telling you. The business really is a lot for you to manage all on your own. Maybe you shouldn't have been so quick to turn down the developers when -"

"I do just fine." Hannah can be just as stubborn as her cousin when she wants to be, and with a theatrical sigh, she puts down her patchwork, carefully folding her needle and thread into the center of her quilt and burying the lot in her cavernous purse. "But you're quite right. There's lots to do, and we should both be on hand if James Trainor wants to talk to us. Come along, Jean. What have you been buying?"

"Prepared dishes." Jean snatches the bag out of Hannah's reach. "As none of our guests seem eager to eat any home-cooked food at the moment."

Hannah's eyes fill with tears, and I give her arm a quick squeeze.

"I'm sure things will settle down soon," I say again. "Just as soon as the police work out what really happened." I draw a breath. "Everything will be fine once they confirm that it has nothing to do with anybody at the inn."

Hannah nods, but I can tell from her expression she doesn't believe me. I don't really believe myself. Who else could it have been? *One of the people at the inn - guests, or staff, or somebody - is a killer. And nobody is going to feel safe there until we figure out who.* I check my watch and decide I can afford a fifteen-minute break to see the two cousins safely home. *And maybe, while I'm there, I'll manage a little investigating of my own...*

Chapter Nine

By the time we get back to the Harmony Inn, the bickering between the two cousins has reached an all-out war.

"Hannah, you look exhausted! Why don't you go back to bed?"

"I'm perfectly fine. I don't need you ordering me around in my own house, Jean Montrose!" Hannah turns pointedly in my direction. "And we have guests to look after."

"Don't you worry about me!" I laugh weakly. "Either of you! I'm just going to put all this away in the kitchen and then get out of your hair!" I lift the heavy bags out of the boot of my car and hope I look and sound a lot more innocent than I feel. "Is Anton around?"

"Moping, probably." Jean waves me towards the kitchen. "He's like a sad puppy with nobody to play with."

"And whose fault is that? If you were a little more forceful with the police in explaining his innocence -"

"I did all I could!" Jean protests. "It's not my fault none of the guests want to stay here anymore. They're all afraid they're going to be the next one on the chopping block. I'm not sure we'll ever manage to recover from this. By the way, did you see Edgar is shortening his stay?"

"What?"

I duck away from the squabbling pair, eager not to be drawn into yet another argument. I know Hannah is worried about losing business, but she's going to look heartless if she continues operating as usual in the midst of a murder investigation. I tiptoe into the kitchen, more determined than ever to find a clue or two that might help bring the truth to light. I glance around warily, noticing the almost surgical neatness of the kitchen. It certainly doesn't look like the place a poisoner might work. *Or does it? Perhaps Anton just knows how to clean up after himself...* I shake my head, forcing my thoughts not to lead me down an alley. I have no evidence that the poison originated here in the kitchen and certainly no proof that Anton was responsible. *So maybe it's about time I find some.*

I open the industrial-sized refrigerator and swiftly start unloading ready meals, blinking at the pictures on the front and thinking of the unappetizing dinner I have to look forward to. For a fleeting moment I think about eating out tonight, but then I remember the look of despair on Hannah Kincaid's face as she watched guest after guest desert her business. I can't add to her troubles. *Besides,* I tell myself, trying to be cheerful. *Maybe this Quick'n'Tastee Lasagne al Forno will taste as good as the picture on the box looks!* My nose wrinkles. I doubt it.

Sliding the last few boxed meals into the refrigerator I close the door and lean against it, peering around the kitchen and wondering where I should begin my search. I can hear the low rumble of voices elsewhere in the inn which suggests the war of the Montrose-Kincaids is still ongoing and I won't be missed for a little while yet. There's never going to be another chance like this one.

"Oh, just start looking," I mutter aloud, crossing the room and yanking open a drawer. An unsuspicious tray of clean, sparkling cutlery greets me and I roll my eyes, closing it and reaching for the one next door, then check the two cupboards underneath. Apart from a few old but spotless casserole dishes I don't see anything suspicious until I reach a cupboard stuffed to the gills with little spice jars. *Jackpot!* I shuffle the jars around, trying to decipher handwritten labels and in the end resort to removing lids and sniffing, and wishing I was better at identifying herbs and spices by their smell.

"What do you think you're doing?"

I gasp, breathing in a great powdery lungful of something that burns the insides of my nose and makes me sneeze.

"I'm-I'm sorry!" I blurt, in between bouts of sneezing, and reach up to wipe the tears out of my eyes. I haven't been careful enough with my handling of the spice jars, though, and something on my fingertips makes its way into my eyes, which scream with stinging pain. "Water!" I manage, fumbling blindly towards the sink. I cup handfuls of cold water with my hands and rinse my eyes and at last I'm sane enough to turn towards the man who made me jump in the first place.

"Anton?"

"This is my kitchen!" He glares at me. "Guests are not allowed in 'ere!"

His accent changes as he speaks, lapsing in and out of the sort of exaggerated French that belongs in a cartoon and it takes me a while to form a response.

"I was putting some things away," I say, defensively. "For Hannah and Jean." I fold my arms across my front, noticing too late that I'm covered in traces of different powdered spices. I draw in a ragged breath and hope I look more composed than I feel. "You can ask them."

"And did they tell you to go poking around in my cupboards, making a mess of everything?" He stalks over to the spice cabinet and reaches inside, muttering to himself as he tries to restore order. "First the police, now you!"

"The police?"

"They came and searched everything." He swallows and I see his hand shaking as he finally closes the cupboard door. "Thinking I had something to do with what happened to Delphine. Me!" His eyes narrow as he fixes them on me. "I suppose you thought so too, huh? Blame the -"

"This has nothing to do with you being French." I'm not about to be labeled a racist on top of everything else.

"I was going to say *ex-convict*." His accent has completely disappeared now, and he runs a hand over his head, sliding his chef's cap off. "Well, I guess at least one person here didn't know all about my shameful past." He smiles ruefully as he sees the shock I haven't even tried to hide. "I thought the secret was already out there for everybody to know. It's only a matter of time in this place." He jerks his head towards the door and I'm not sure if by *this place* he means the inn or Silver Brook as a whole. I love my town, but with everybody in everyone else's business, it certainly isn't easy to keep a secret. *Which Anton seems to have managed pretty well up to now.* "Sit down," he says, with a sigh. "I'll make us something to drink." His hand hovers over the kettle, then he reaches instead for a half-drunk bottle of wine. "I guess it's five o'clock somewhere." He pours a healthy glug of merlot into two glasses and cheerses them himself before passing one to me and I stare at it, not sure how I seem to have stumbled into an episode of the Twilight Zone.

"My name isn't really Anton." He's the first to speak, and without the affected French accent, his voice sounds deeper and more measured. "It's Anthony. Tony. And this?" He gestures to his chef's apron. "I learned in the slammer." He smiles a crooked smile. "No conservatoire classes for me."

"Do Hannah and Jean know?"

He hesitates.

"They didn't before all this. I guess they will now. I'm handing in my notice. Can't expect to keep my job once they know I lied to get it." He sighs. "And there aren't that many people looking to hire a chef involved in a poisoning case."

"Involved?" I turn, trying to gauge which of us is closer to the door.

"I didn't do it," he says again. "And before you ask, I was locked up for dodgy bookkeeping. Nothing violent." He grins but the effect is so menacing I'm not exactly reassured. "This was meant to be my fresh start. It would've been too, if it wasn't for Delphine and her spy games."

"What? What spy games?" I put down my glass of wine without drinking it and turn to face him.

"Well she knew I wasn't French, to start with." He sighs. "She had a lot of fun holding that secret over me for as long as she could. And she was always sticking her nose into things, going through guests' belongings and learning their secrets." He nods at me. "I'd check my bags if I were you. She liked to help herself to things, too."

My hand goes straight to one of my earrings, the pair I thought I'd lost only for Hannah to find them on the floor of her room. I shudder, wondering if they had been in the possession of a dead girl.

"Delphine knew all sorts of things," Anton continues, growing serious all at once. "I can't have been the only one around here keeping a secret. And now I wonder if that's what got her killed."

Chapter Ten

"There! It took some effort but I finally convinced my cousin to -"

Jean stops talking as she enters the kitchen and sees me standing there, deep in conversation with Anton, who hastily hides his glass of wine and turns to greet his boss with something that might have been a bow.

"Merry!" I can hear the tension in Jean's voice as she turns to me. "What are you still doing here?"

"I was just leaving," I say, hurrying towards the door. A look passes between Jean and Anton and I wonder if she's as oblivious to his true identity as he claims. "How is Hannah doing now?"

"She's gone upstairs to rest at last." Jean strides towards the stove and checks the kettle, before firing up the burner and putting it on to boil. "I said I'd bring some tea up for her myself - that way she could be certain it wouldn't be tampered with." She smiles at me. "Would you like a cup?"

"I really ought to get going," I say, turning back towards the door. "But I might run up and say goodbye."

"You don't need to!" Jean says. "She's very tired. I think she'll probably already be asleep."

I'm already climbing the stairs and stop only when Chris meets me coming the other way.

"Merry!" She smiles. "I was just on my way to visit you at the Jitterbug!" Her smile drops. "What's wrong? Aren't you working today?"

"I'm just about to go back," I say. "I just need to say goodbye to Hannah first."

"Is she still not feeling well?" Chris frowns. "I'll stop in with you." She beats me to the door, pushing it open, and then freezes so that I end up walking right into her.

"Ouch!"

"Hannah?" I can hear the note of concern in Chris's voice, and she hurries over to the bed, bending over the figure lying prone on top of the blankets.

"Is she sleeping?" I ask, sliding my purse back up my arm from where our collision knocked it off. "Hannah?" I soften my voice, then see what Chris has already noticed. Hannah isn't sleeping. Her eyes are wide open, staring upwards into nothing.

• • • •

"NOW, MERRY." CHIEF Trainor runs a weary hand through his thinning hair and looks at me. "Why don't you tell me what happened?" An edge comes into his voice. "And just how you happened to be on the scene for *this* death?"

I bite my lip to keep from answering back. There's something I don't like about his tone, but me being irritable isn't going to help my case.

"I was working at the Jitterbug today," I begin, folding my hands in my lap. "But you know I'm staying here while I get my house fumigated."

"Yes, Bill Hughes confirmed that."

I feel my eyebrows tug together. *Bill confirmed. Like my word wasn't good enough?* Again, I fight the urge to tell Trainor a home truth or two. I'm sure he doesn't mean to sound like he suspects me of being involved, but without Kate here on the scene or even in town, I'm starting to feel like he'd happily pin it on me just out of spite.

"I'm staying here while I get my house fumigated," I repeat. "But today I was at work when Jean and Hannah stopped in. They were running errands. They had some heavy bags of shopping and I offered to help them bring them back." I swallow and force the sweetest smile I can summon onto my face. "You can check with Anton if you like. He was with me in the kitchen." *There,* I think, watching the slightest hint of a frown darken the police chief's forehead as he jots that important detail down. *I have an alibi.* And so does Anton, for what it's worth. *Although I guess he's off the hook now that there's been another death.* My stomach turns over. *A non-poisoning death.* I remember Hannah's wide, sightless eyes and draw in a shaky breath.

"Do you know how she died?"

"Unconfirmed." Chief Trainor glances at his watch. "I'm waiting for the hospital to call. It could be natural causes, but after what happened to Delphine..."

"Right."

"So you were in the kitchen with Anton. And then what happened?"

"I was on my way back to work. Jean came into the kitchen and said that Hannah was still not feeling well and had gone back to bed so I ran up to check on her and say goodbye before I left."

"And that's when you saw Chris?"

"That's right." I watch as he flips back through his notes. He's already spoken to Chris, so I'm fairly sure her account will match mine. "She went into the room first, and she seemed to have a handle on things a lot quicker than I did." I sniff, feeling tears prick at the corners of my eyes. I can't believe I was ever suspicious of Hannah. All this time I was wondering if she might have been a murderer - and now she's a victim! *Not necessarily a victim*, I remind myself. *There's every chance this could have been a natural death. Brought on by stress, no doubt.*

"That's fine." I'm so lost in my thoughts Trainor has to repeat himself a second time before I catch the dismissal in his voice. "I'm sure it was quite a shock, coming across Ms. Kincaid like this. We always think people will go on living forever, but she's been suffering for quite some time, according to her cousin. Try not to let it upset you too much." He grimaces at me and I'm so startled it takes me a minute to understand he's trying to smile. He's trying to be nice. I nod, thinking that Kate will never believe me when I tell her that her boss seems to have grown a heart while she's been away.

"If there is a chance something happened to cause this," I begin, my voice little more than a whisper. "You will ensure you find out who's responsible, won't you?" I don't have to tell him I'm not too keen about staying here if there's still a murderer on the loose. *Even if Hannah died of natural causes, that still doesn't explain what happened to Delphine.* I swallow past a lump in my throat. "Jean must be so worried."

"She's handling the situation a lot better than I anticipated." Trainor shakes his head. "I mean, obviously, she's devastated at the loss of her cousin. They were very close, you know."

Now it's my turn to shake my head. *Very close?* They spent their whole time together bickering.

"And she's Hannah's only family, so this whole place will come to her now." He smiles, sadly. "The last of the Kincaids."

"Montrose," I correct.

"Only by marriage. Once a Kincaid, always a Kincaid." Trainor hauls himself out of his chair. "Only I don't suppose she'll keep it as an inn for much longer. Developers have been sniffing around this place for years. I expect she'll make a tidy sum selling the land. Much more than it would have brought in like this." He sees my expression change and instantly misunderstands it, chuckling softly. "Oh, don't worry. She certainly won't do anything right away. No, no. You're quite safe here." He seems to hear the implication of his words and grows serious. "Quite safe. I want to track down that other couple that were staying here. They scarpered out of town pretty quickly. Mighty suspicious if you ask me. I've already put in a call with other local police departments though and I'm sure we'll be able to track them down. You needn't worry, Merry. Keeping the rest of the Harmony Inn guests safe is my top priority. I'll post an officer here overnight." He rubs at his deep frown lines. "It'd help if we weren't a man down, but with Kate away..."

"Thank you," I say, wanting time to myself to digest an idea that's starting to form at the edge of my mind. "If you don't need me any more I had better get back to work. I only meant to be gone a few minutes."

"Sure thing." A movement by the door catches his eye and he straightens in his chair, becoming oddly formal. "How are you, Jean?"

I glance over my shoulder and see a white-faced Jean smiling tiredly in my direction.

"I wondered if you could give me a ride back into town, Merry, dear. There are a few things I forgot to pick up on my errand run this morning."

"Now?" I can't hide my surprise. "Are you sure? I'd be more than happy to do anything you need. You don't have to go anywhere."

"That's so kind." Jean shakes her head, firm in her decision. "But honestly, I could do with a little time to myself. I want to clear my head. Everything's happened so...so quickly."

I glance at Trainor, who is reading back over his notes and seems to be in no hurry to leave his seat.

"Well, sure." I stand and follow Jean out of the inn to the small parking area where I left my car.

Chapter Eleven

"**A**re you sure you want to be out and about at a time like this?"

Jean hasn't said a word since she climbed into my car and when I look back at her, she is still very pale. Her lips are pressed together in a thin line and she's gripping her knees so tightly her knuckles stick out.

"I think I ought to take you back to the inn," I say, checking my rearview mirror before hitting my turn signal and turning the car around. "You've had a shock." I pause, remembering Delphine. "Two shocks. And I don't think you should be alone right now."

"But I'm not alone." Jean's voice is strangely high-pitched, cheerful in that forced way that a game show host is. I look at her again and this time she smiles, but the effect is entirely disconcerting. "If you're determined to take me back to the inn then at least let's go the pretty way." She points me towards a turn off the main road and nods enthusiastically until I take it, wincing as my car bounces onto a gravel track. "This is the old road to the Kincaid property from long back before it was the Harmony Inn." She reaches up to smooth a loose grey curl into place. "Do you know what the Kincaid's place used to be, back in the day?"

"No," I say, even though I can hear Edgar's voice in my head describing various misdeeds attributed to previous Harmony Inn residents and owners.

"It was quite shocking. A house of ill-repute if you can believe that." She clucks her tongue. "The Kincaids have quite a chequered past. Not like now, of course. My dear cousin would never want anyone to know the truth of where we came from. Not when she can put a sheen of respectability over it. And chintz." She grimaces. "Of course, I think the whole place ought to have been torn down years ago. And now, just as soon as the estate is settled, it will be." She lets out a relieved sigh, and when I glance at her she's staring out of the window, her gaze fixed on the horizon.

"I'm not sure there's a path here anymore, Jean," I say, as my car lurches from one ditch to another, jogging us from side to side. "Maybe I should go back to the road."

"No!" Jean's hand reaches for the steering wheel before I can stop her. "We're taking the scenic route." She's insistent now. "After all, don't you want to know where all the bodies are buried?"

A cold shiver runs up my back and I ease off the gas, letting the car roll to a stop.

"I'm joking!" Jean laughs, forcing me to catch her eye. "No, you don't need to worry, dear. There are no bodies. Not anymore." She blinks. "Of course, if my cousin had done the decent thing and sold the place when I asked her to, she'd still be alive to enjoy her half of our inheritance."

The moment of ease I'd felt when I thought Jean was joking - strange, sinister joking, but joking all the same - vanishes, and before I can say a word she lunges at me, her thin, bony hands knotting tightly around my neck.

· · · ·

SHE'S SURPRISINGLY strong for such a little woman, helped, of course, by the fact that she's caught me by surprise. My foot sinks down on the gas, making the car lurch forward, and as I try to fight her off I turn the steering wheel, praying the car will find another of those unfortunate potholes I can use to my advantage. We jerk to the left and the motion is enough to loosen Jean's grip on my neck not by much, but enough that I can shove her away from me. I can hear dogs barking and wonder where on earth she's brought me to, but I don't have time to think. She's fumbling with her seatbelt but I'm quicker and I throw open my door, flinging myself out into the dirt. The engine is still running but I don't slow down. I scramble to my feet and run, and then I hear footsteps running towards me and a voice that sounds oddly familiar.

"Merry?"

"Chris?" I turn, and two huge hairy, barking monsters fly at me, followed by Chris, who does her best to wrangle the dogs off me.

"I thought that was you! What are you doing here?" She sees my expression and grows serious immediately, directing the dogs to sit. I'm surprised by how quickly they obey but there's something so commanding about her voice that I almost drop back to the ground myself. "What happened to you?" Chris asks, taking a step closer to me.

"J-Jean!" I wheeze, pointing behind me to where I abandoned my vehicle. "Car...hurt..." I'm down to single words and even those aren't particularly helpful. A painful stitch in my side folds me over in the middle and I gulp in air, flinching when Chris lays a hand on my back.

"Merry, what happened?" There's that commanding tone again, the one that instantly makes me feel like obeying.

"Jean's the killer," I manage at last. "She tried to strangle me!"

Chris steps in front of me, blocking my view of the road, and that's when I see Jean coming towards us.

"Christine! Oh, dear! You have to help us! Poor Meredith seems to have had a funny turn in the car just now..."

"Stay where you are, please," Chris is blocking me now, with her body, and I hear a low growl that it takes me a moment to identify. I drop my gaze. The dogs have turned so that they, too, are between me and Chris, and Jean. They're tense and ready to spring into action at the slightest direction and that's when I remember what Rob told me his friend is really doing in Silver Brook. *She's a K-9 police dog trainer. Coming to work with me on some new recruits for her department in the city.* "Merry?" Chris isn't looking at me, but her voice calls my attention. "Did you say Jean tried to hurt you?"

"She did." I press a hand against the thin scratches on my neck. "And she killed Hannah. Delphine too," I add, although I'm only guessing at that.

"Delphine was an accident." Jean abandons the act, seeing in an instant that she isn't fooling either of us. "That tea was meant for my dear cousin. Old Nanna Kincaid's family recipe." She smiles, that same cold, sinister smile I saw in the car. "Just a few drops of her special potion in a cup of tea. Sweetens it, y'see, so the unwitting drinker will think it's just sugar." She frowns. "I didn't expect it to have such a quick effect on dear old Delphine, but I guess there's no accounting for personal differences." She looks down at the dogs, who are still rigidly glaring at her. "But there's no proof of any of this. Unless you think these two will count as expert witnesses."

"They don't need to."

A male voice that I can't quite place floats up from the road and it's enough to disorient Jean, who turns her head to see Edgar approaching us. He's tapping furiously into his phone as he walks, and I hear Chris whisper something soothing to the two dogs at our feet, who obediently relax.

"What are you doing here?" Jean spits.

"Research." Edgar smiles, and I'm surprised at how much it improves him. He slides his glasses up his nose, the same gesture I've seen him do a hundred times before. "I've been studying the Kincaid family and its shady past, and just up here is the old smugglers' cellar." His smile drops. "It looks like the family propensity for crime didn't die out generations ago after all."

"Jean Montrose." Chris steps forward, securing both of Jean's thin wrists with one hand. "You're under arrest for murder."

Chapter Twelve

"**A**re you sure we can't persuade you to stick around?"

Trainor is congratulating Chris on a job well done and I can tell he'd be more than happy to add her to his staff permanently. I wonder what Kate would make of the competition, but Chris is quick to talk herself out of a job offer.

"You're very kind, but I've got these two to take care of." She stoops and scratches one of her two dogs behind their ears. "I'm sure you don't have much need for police dogs in a sweet little town like Silver Brook."

"No, you're quite right." Trainor glances down at the dogs and shuffles a little away from them, his apparent nerves making Chris keep a tight hold on both dogs' leashes. "Well, I'd better get to the station. I need to get Jean's statement on record, although from what you and Merry have said, and Edgar's, ah, detailed summary, we should have more than enough to make a case against her."

"Good!" Chris looks my way. "But it's all thanks to Merry. If she hadn't gotten the truth out of Jean..."

"Yes, Merry has a habit of persuading people to confess to their crimes." Trainor smiles wearily in my direction, then bids both of us a farewell before swiftly striding away.

"I think that was almost a compliment, Merry," Chris says, stifling a laugh.

"I think it's about as close as I'm ever going to get, where Jim Trainor is concerned." I bend down and stroke the dog nearest me, then wince as the scratches on my neck catch on the collar of my shirt.

"You should put some cream on those scratches. Come on, I have something that should help." Chris loops the dog leashes over a pole and stops to instruct the dogs to remain where they are. As if they understand, both of them obediently lie down, content to await further instructions.

"You are amazing with them," I say, as we head back into the inn.

"I should be!" Chris sighs. "They take enough out of me. But I'm glad I had them with me today. I'm not sure Jean would have backed down so easily without my four-legged backup."

"You shouldn't talk about Edgar like that." We exchange a look and are both laughing as we step into the inn and are immediately pounced on by Anton.

"Good! You're both still here." He's dropped every hint of French accent and instead of wearing his starched white chef's uniform, he's dressed informally in jeans and a t-shirt. He looks lighter than I've ever seen him and after a minute I realize why. He's smiling. "I'm hoping you can help me out." He's looking at me, and I glance nervously at Chris, who is as nonplussed as I am.

"With what?"

"I need to find a job. I hear there are only a couple of restaurants in Silver Brook, and I'm hoping the owner of the best cafe in town will help me out."

"The only cafe in town," Chris puts in, in an undertone suspiciously pitched to remind me of Edgar's persistent fact-checking.

"I'd love to help you." I wince. "But I'm not exactly in a position to be hiring new staff right now..."

"Oh, I'm not asking you for a job." Anton's smile widens and I begin to wonder why I ever thought he was intimidating. He's a teddy bear. "But maybe you could help me out with an endorsement? If I'm expecting to work at Pierre's I don't think he's going to care for my fake French chef impression, do you?" He pulls a face, and Chris and I laugh, pleased to feel the tension of the last few days ease at last.

"I think we can figure something out."

He offers each of us an arm, and as a trio we walk into the sitting room of the inn, eager to plan for a future far away from this place.

• • • •

I MEET ROB A FEW DAYS later for a dog-walking date - he has his two, and I've offered to walk Chris's two charges, which makes for a quartet of chaos we just about manage to keep control of.

"Who's running the inn now?" he asks, as we round the corner of the Silver Brook high street and make our way back towards the Jitterbug Junction. "I mean, there's still a few of you staying there, right?"

"Yes." I sigh. I can't wait to get back to living under my own roof, but as I suspected Bill the Bug Guy's "it'll take about a week" promise was too good to be true. He is making progress, slowly, and I'm doing my best to be patient. It isn't easy, now that staying at the inn has become *helping to run it*. "It's a bit of a free-for-all," I admit. "But between me, Chris, and Anton we're just about managing to keep things moving. Edgar is less than helpful, except in the constructive-criticism department."

Rob clears his throat before pointing at something I haven't noticed yet. There, in the window of Peter Stalker's bookstore, I see Edgar engaged in a very serious-looking discussion with Silver Brook's favorite bookseller.

"What do you reckon that's about?" he asks, yanking on one of his dog leashes to pull his more adventurous pup into line.

"They'll be publishing a criminal history of Silver Brook, I expect." I roll my eyes. "With a special additional chapter about the murders at the Harmony Inn. I'm sure with Edgar writing it there won't be a single detail missed out." I pause. "Except for Dan and Sally's next stop on the romantic nostalgia tour of small-town America." I shake my head. "They were a strange pair."

"They were sweet. Nothing wrong with trying to recapture the magic." Rob grins. "Though I'd love to know what they told Jim Trainor to get them off his list of potential suspects so quickly. I think you and I were both under suspicion for longer than they were, and he actually knows us!"

"Yeah, but he only likes you." I take another look at Edgar's pitch meeting with Peter and wonder just what his book will have to say about me, if anything. *As long as he says something nice about the Jitterbug Junction, I'll be happy.*

"I hope he remembers to give you a cut of the royalties for your starring role in bringing down the killer," Rob leans over and kisses me. "Although I'm beginning to get a little worried about you. It's one thing to have an unfortunate habit of tripping over dead bodies -"

"Um, you've had almost as much bad luck as I have on that front," I remind him, and he acknowledges the point with a nod.

"But I don't tend to wind up going toe-to-toe with murderers." He grows serious all of a sudden. "You could have been badly hurt, Mer."

I tug at the scarf I'm wearing to cover up the faint bruises that remain from Jean's vice-like grip around my throat.

"It all turned out just fine," I remind him, before bending to stroke one of my four-legged rescuers. "All thanks to these two. And Chris of course." I sigh, realizing how much I'll miss my new friend - and her two furry companions - when they leave town. "How long before she goes?"

"A couple of days." Rob smiles. "It's been so great having her here, but she's back off to the city to put these guys to work."

"Maybe she can come back and visit sometime. You know she still hasn't tried any of the Jitterbug's most popular pastries."

"Well, that's certainly an oversight we need to remedy." Rob whistles, and all four dogs leap to attention. "Maybe we can get her to meet us there now, and you can whip us up a fresh batch."

"Oh, I can, can I?"

"If I recall, you didn't trust me in the kitchen when I volunteered to help out," Rob reminds me, pressing a kiss to my cheek. "But I'm more than happy to eat my fill." He hesitates. "Providing you haven't got any ideas from your stay at the Harmony Inn."

"You mean you don't want croissants baked by ze Frenchest of French chefs?" I put on an exaggerated version of Anton's accent, and Rob rolls his eyes.

"I don't think even *Pierre*'s pastries can compete with yours. Maybe you'll teach me sometime?"

"In case you want a career change? I don't know, it could get kind of messy, dating, working together..."

"Living together?" Rob asks the question in such an easy, light-hearted manner that I miss it at first, but when I look at him there's a gleam in his eyes that suggests he's serious.

"All things in good time," I say, and we stay in step all the way back to the cafe, talking happily about how bright our future looks.

• • • •

The End

About the Author

When Rachel Beattie[1] isn't writing stories, she's usually reading them - especially of the cozy mystery variety. A lifelong devotee of Agatha Christie, she loves putting ze little grey cells to work and is especially fond of anything that can make her laugh while she's collecting a clue or two.

• • • •

She regularly shares updates, news and progress on stories she's writing for on Ream[2] – as well as a host of other bonuses. Become a free follower for more information.

---

1. https://reamstories.com/rachelbeattiewrites

2. https://reamstories.com/rachelbeattiewrites

Milton Keynes UK
Ingram Content Group UK Ltd.
UKHW030635071024
449371UK00001B/55

9 798227 321251